In addition to writing, Norma Farber
has also been a concert singer,
actress, and poet. After receiving her
B.A. from Wellesley College and her
M.A. from Radcliffe, she studied
singing in Belgium. She has also lived
in Germany and Switzerland.

She is the mother of four children,
two sons and two daughters, and has
three grandchildren.

Carole Vizbara is a graduate of
Pratt Institute. She has designed
greeting cards, and much of her work
has been used in magazines and
advertising. "For fun" she says, she
has recently created a small boutique
line called Kara Creations, which she
works on when she finds some
free time.

She and her husband are now in the
process of building a house in
Vermont, which they have designed
themselves with the help of an
architect.

DID YOU KNOW
IT WAS
THE
NARWHALE?

DID
YOU KNOW
IT WAS
THE
NARWHALE?

NORMA FARBER

ILLUSTRATED BY
CAROLE VIZBARA

ATHENEUM
NEW YORK 1967

For Wendy, Peter, Billy.

Did you know it was the Unicorn,

bounding through the wood,

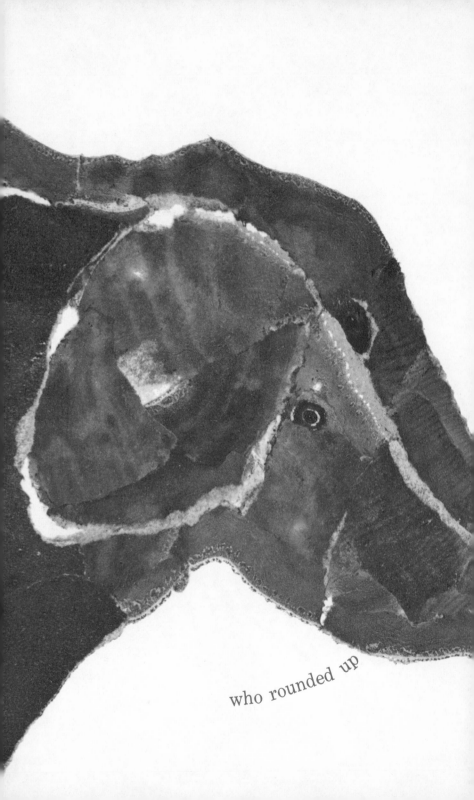

who rounded up

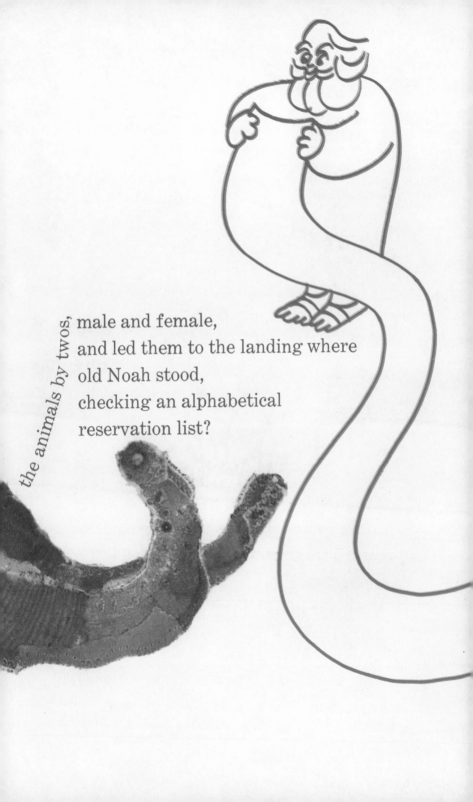

the animals by twos, male and female,
and led them to the landing where
old Noah stood,
checking an alphabetical
reservation list?

Did you know it was the Unicorn
who kept that teeming shipload of paired
passengers
from pushing up the gangway
out of order?

He it was who set to work two busy Beavers,
to build a willow-turnstile on the dock.
He took up watch beside it,
and nimbly with his horn, and neatly,
kept prodding whoso tried to leap the bars,
or scuttle under:

a pair of Goats, for instance, whom he sent—
as an example to all others—
the whole long distance to the rear,
clear to the

Zebra tail-end of the line.

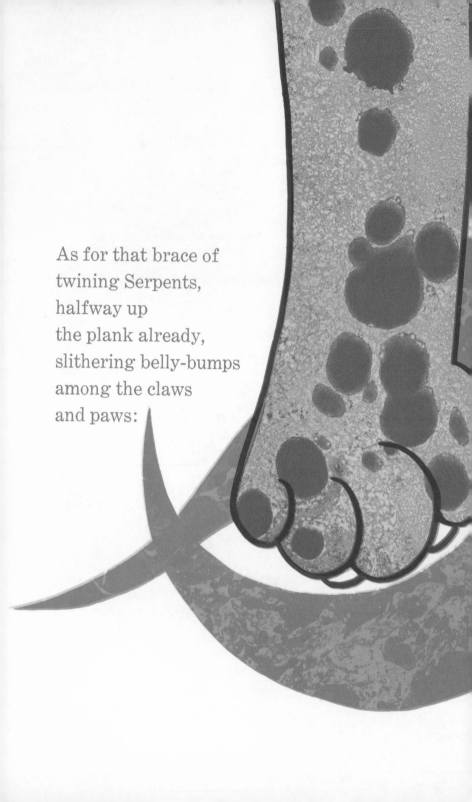

As for that brace of
twining Serpents,
halfway up
the plank already,
slithering belly-bumps
among the claws
and paws:

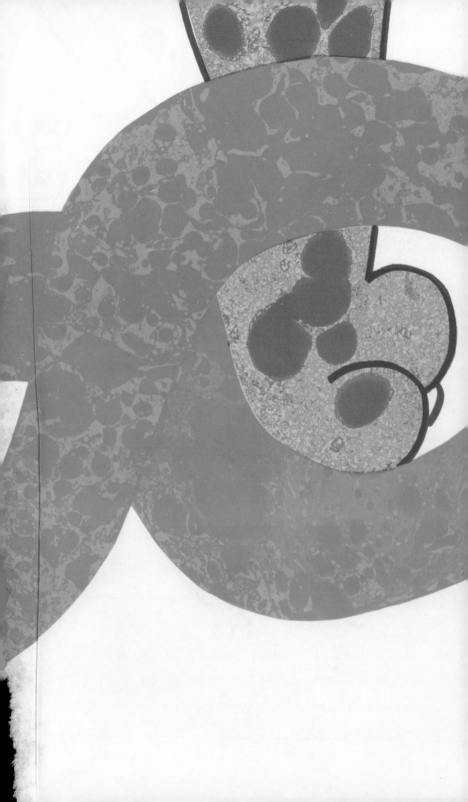

first he poked them to a stop,
with his white horn-point.
Then he nodded toward the *s*'s,
where the Shrews, the Slugs,
the Squirrels queued
quietly as they should.

He picked those Serpents up in the air,
twisted them round his horn securely,
cantered a hundred yards or so,
came to a stop,

and put the pair
between the curious
Scorpions and the

Sheep.

And everyone in due course
boarded the Ark.

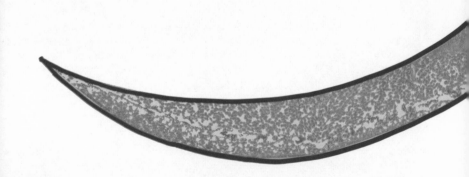

(Including an extra,
pocket-hidden Kangaroo-kin,
too tiny to be counted.)

Did you know it was the Unicorn
who did the casting off,
when the last of the beasts
had been tightly accommodated
in the final crowded corner of the poop?
He loosened all the cables.
He tossed them to old Noah.
He stayed and watched the vessel
as it groaned away uneasy
from the bumpers on the pilings.

"Did you know I've left a lifebuoy on the stern?"
cried old Noah.
"I can't take you on board,
very sorry, not an inch to spare.
Besides, you're only single, just one Unicorn,
a bachelor.
You have to be in pairs to be my passengers.
I have my written orders.
But put the belt around you,
and paddle along behind us.

You can rest your horn from time to time
in someone's lap or other,
who's handy at the rail.
Stay with the crowd, be saved with us.
The pleasure's mine to have you trail a-stern.
You've loaded up my ballast like a pro.
Stay with the crowd, be welcome.
And when we reach some distant port or other,
you'll help me disembark us two by two,
most alphabetically."

Did you know that forty days and nights
the Unicorn hung on behind the Ark?
The life-buoy made the voyage somewhat easier.
And every now and then,
he laid the spiral ivory of his horn
between a Camel's humps
(the creature knelt convenient by the rail),

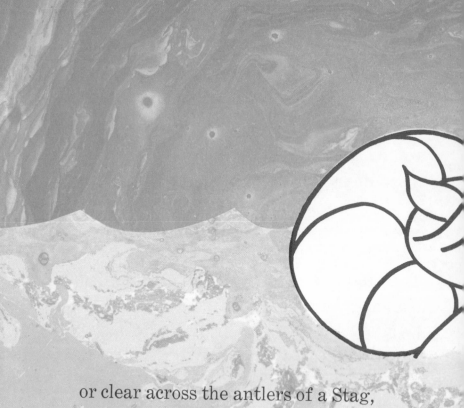

or clear across the antlers of a Stag,
who lay there statue-still,
not to jostle from its resting-place
the pure white shaft.

Did you know that forty days can seem forever

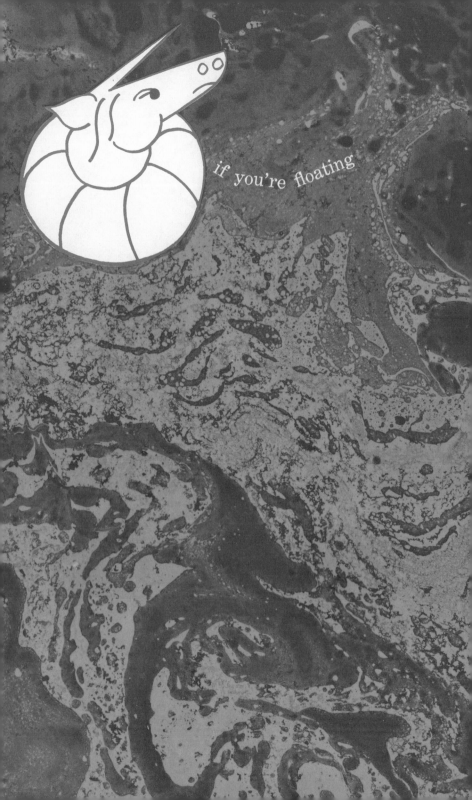

if you're floating

in the wake of an overloaded Ark?
And forty nights forever multiplied?
The Unicorn grew wretched in all that dampness,
all those waters.
Can you blame him?
His coat was sopping wet,
the skin between his toes a wrinkled web—
although he rested them,
one pastern at a time,
on the braided rim of lifebuoy.
He had to hold his chin way up,
or else his nostrils dipped below the surface,
and he sneezed.

Did you know the woods had long since drowned
within his weary watery memory,
deep as ever they perished under the flood?
His hooves could pound no springing earth.
His nose could smell no fragrant,
trampled balsam needles.
His mouth tasted no tart young shoots.
He rested in no shadows
where a friendly sun played hide-and-seek.
The waves, slap-slapping,
scuttled the last leaf-rustle
out of his ears.
He sucked a limp green water-weed,
not with much appetite.
No solid succulence to sink one's teeth into.

Did you know a white Beluga Whale,
that morning of the fortieth day,
came swimming up beside him?
"I'll keep you company," she said.
And "Easy does it, Cousin.
Let go the lifebuoy, once for all.
Just let your flippers take you
where you're going."

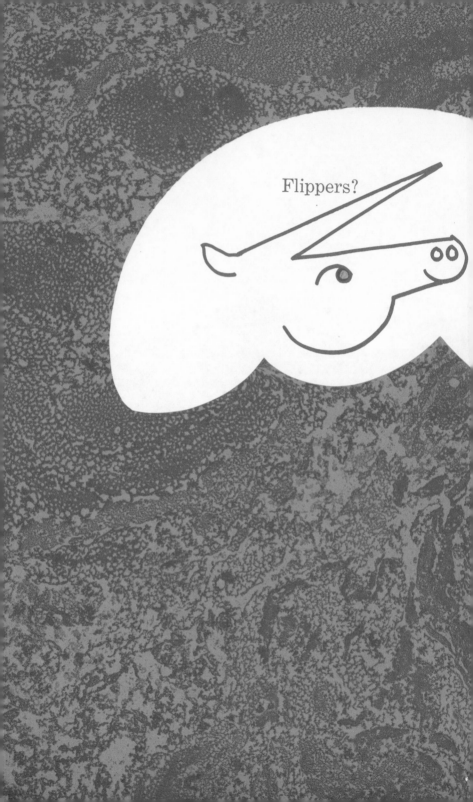

Flippers!

No knee, no shank, no hoof at all!

Did you know he looked to right and left—
that flabbergasted onetime Unicorn—
and found he had two flippers:
one flapping from each side of his sleek person?
What else?
A tail, of sorts, at the extreme end
of a long, white whale of body.
No mane, not a single lock.
(A good thing, too. It used to bother him,
drifting into his eyes.)

Did you know
he didn't mind at all,
finding himself so changed?
Was glad, in fact.
Swam like a fish.
No awkward limbs.
Those hind legs gone completely, good!
His courage grew with every flipper-stroke.
He dove way down, shot up, and tried his
blow-hole.
"You called me Cousin.
Did you mean—?"
Still shy, a little.
"Of course," Beluga said.
"We're relatives.
The Whale family, very
distinguished.
Mammals, you know, and all
of that.
You're quite the handsomest,
can't deny it:
the only fish with a horn.
Come on, let's play!"

Did you know they spent the afternoon,
those two, Beluga and Cousin Narwhale,
diving under the Ark, and round and about it,
chasing each other like sun and shadow?
They looped the loop,
stopped on a dime,

then stood straight up like soldiers at attention.

Noah at the helm caught glimpses of happy frolic.
He chuckled as one or the other
came up to the surface
for air—not often.

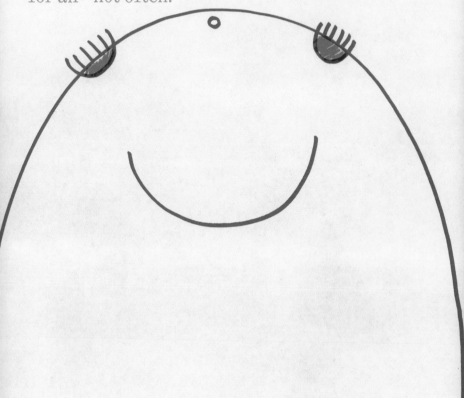

Did you know that on the forty-first of days,

bright and early,

when Ararat, the mountain,
loomed up handy,

and every creature cheered to see a harbor
and dry earth,
and shouted, "Come and see it!"—
did you know the Narwhale found afloat
around him
a whole entire seething pod of family Narwhales:
a lovely hornless female
surrounded by a lively brood,
with horns of every length from small to medium?
All those animals in the Ark
who had crowded to the bow
to watch the wonder of the mountain,
now shoved in the opposite direction
to see that Narwhale marvel in the stern.
"A just reward!" old Noah cried.
"You'll never swim alone again!
Hello. Goodbye.
You Narwhales belong in the Arctic.
Be on your way!"

So off they went with a frisk of tails.

And feeling gladder than he could express,
old Noah let his passengers unload themselves
as wildly
as they wished,
by twos and threes
and countless families,
over and under and through the deck-rails,
by leap and lunge and hurtle,
from port-hole and crow's nest,
by somersault and scamper,
from wheel and mast and rigging,
beyond all rules of alphabetical regulation.

Two wonders in one day called for a celebration.